For Rossella, Camilla, and Paola, for their friendship—B. A.

Copyright © 2002 by Éditions Autrement Jeunesse.
First published in France under the title *Mon Amour*.
English translation copyright © 2005 by North-South Books Inc., New York

All rights reserved. No part of this book may be reproduced or utilized in any form
or by any means, electronic or mechanical, including photocopying, recording, or any
information storage and retrieval system, without permission in writing from the publisher.

First published in the United States, Great Britain, Canada, Australia, and New Zealand
in 2005 by North-South Books, an imprint of NordSüd Verlag AG, Gossau Zürich, Switzerland.
Distributed in the United States by North-South Books Inc., New York.

Library of Congress Cataloging-in-Publication Data is available.
A CIP catalogue record for this book is available from The British Library.
ISBN 0-7358-1993-9 (trade edition) 10 9 8 7 6 5 4 3 2 1
ISBN 0-7358-1994-7 (library edition) 10 9 8 7 6 5 4 3 2 1
Printed in Belgium

For more information about our books, and the authors and artists
who create them, visit our web site: www.northsouth.com

Beatrice Alemagna

My Friend

North-South Books / New York / London

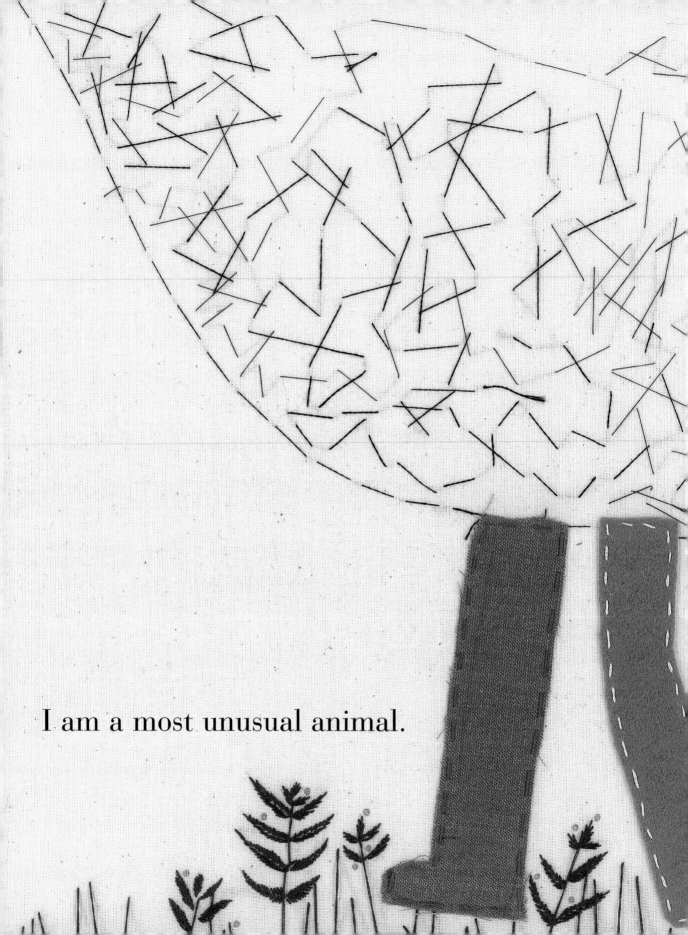

I am a most unusual animal.

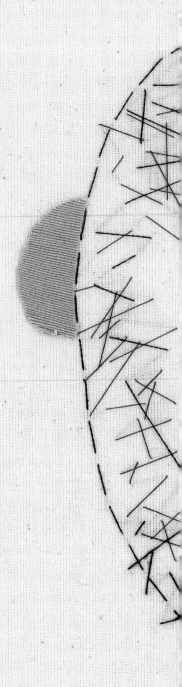

I have fur like a dog and I'm shaped like a sheep.
But no one seems to know just what I am.

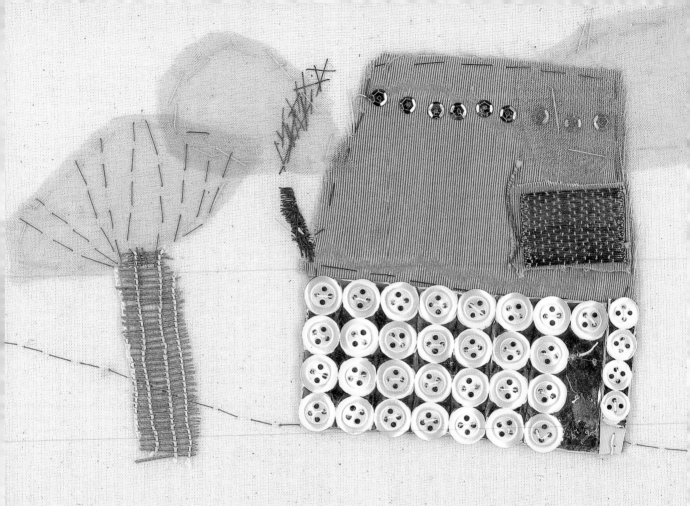

"Hello there, big cat, do you want
to hunt for mice?"

"I'm sorry, but I am not a cat."

"Look at the funny monkey!"

"I am *not* a monkey!"

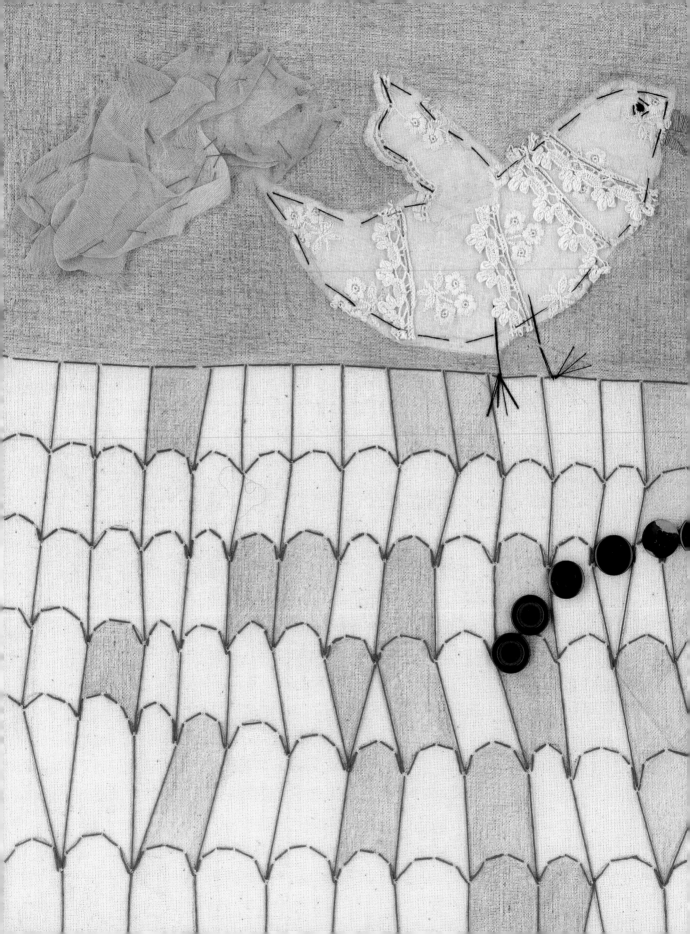

"You must be the lion
I was waiting for!"

"I am not a lion, sir."

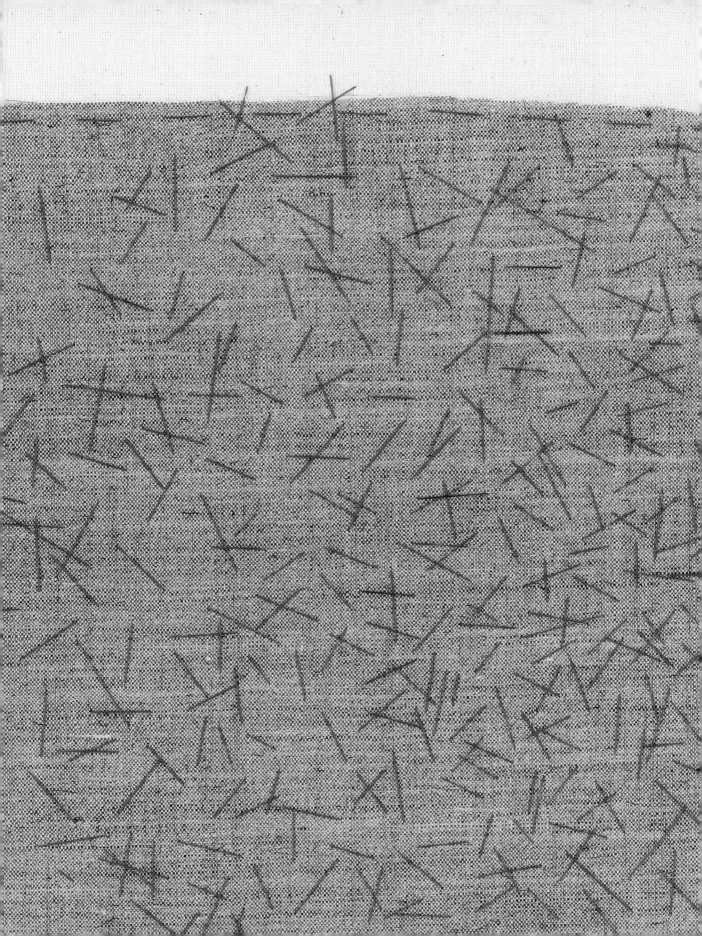

"Great! A furry dog to bite!"

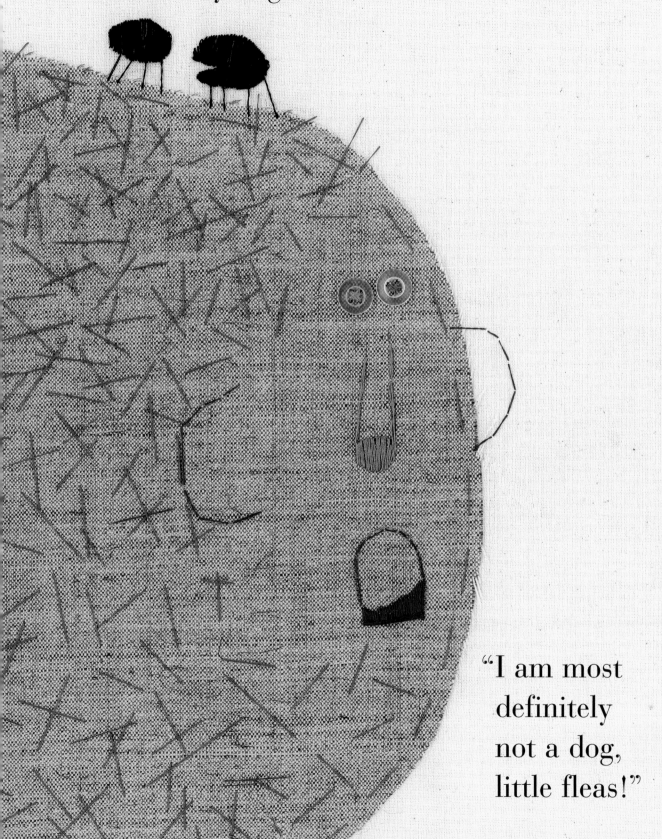

"I am most
definitely
not a dog,
little fleas!"

I am not a crocodile, nor a beaver.
I'm certainly not a hippopotamus.
I am not a mole, nor a wild boar.
But what am I?

"Hello. Do you want to play with me?"

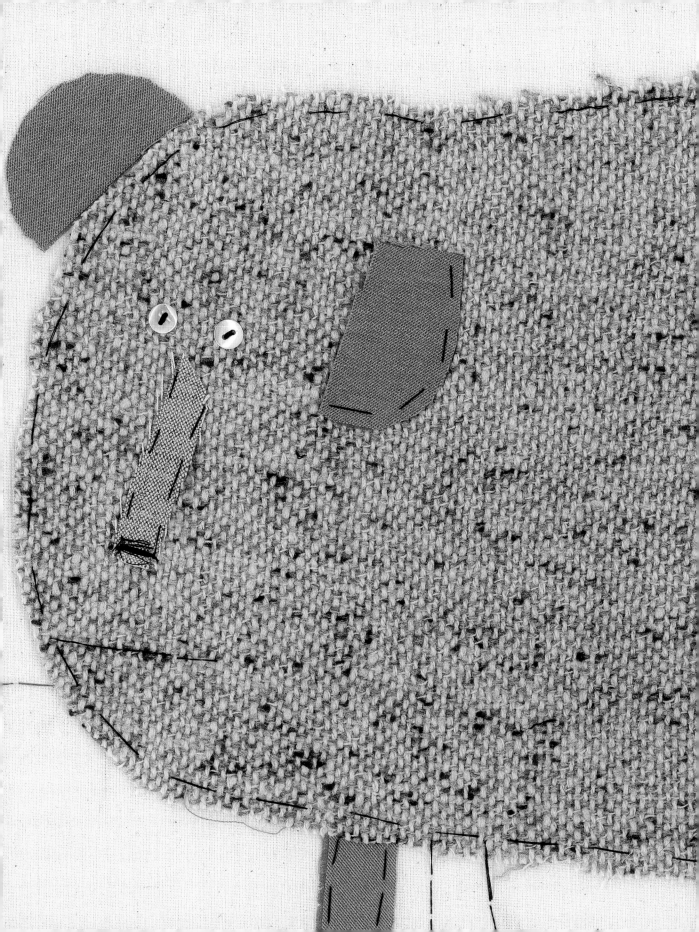

"Don't you
want to know
what I am?"

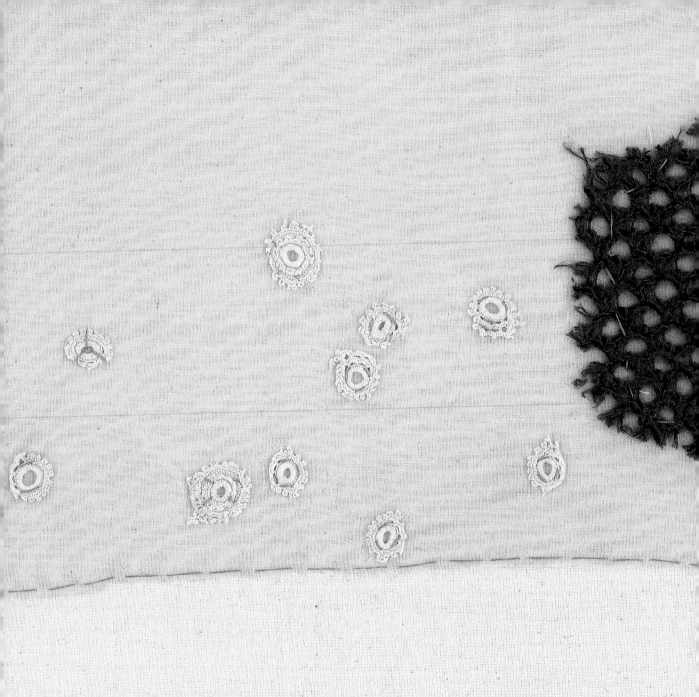

"I know what you are.

You are my friend."